I'll Use Information for My Explanation!

Kelly Doudna

Consulting Editors, Diane Craig, M.A./Reading Specialist
and Susan Kosel, M.A. Education

Published by ABDO Publishing Company, 4940 Viking Drive, Edina, Minnesota 55435.

Printed in the United States.

Credits
Edited by: Pam Price
Curriculum Coordinator: Nancy Tuminelly
Cover and Interior Design and Production: Mighty Media
Photo Credits: AbleStock, BananaStock Ltd., Creatas, Photodisc, ShutterStock, Wewerka Photography

Library of Congress Cataloging-in-Publication Data

Doudna, Kelly, 1963-
    I'll use information for my explanation! / Kelly Doudna.
      p. cm. -- (Science made simple)
    ISBN 10 1-59928-588-6 (hardcover)
    ISBN 10 1-59928-589-4 (paperback)

    ISBN 13 978-1-59928-588-7 (hardcover)
    ISBN 13 978-1-59928-589-4 (paperback)
    1. Research--Juvenile literature. 2. Science--Methodology--Juvenile literature. I. Title. II. Series: Science made simple (ABDO Publishing Company)

    Q180.2D684 2006
    507.2'3--dc22

                                                              2006012565

SandCastle Level: Fluent

SandCastle™ books are created by a professional team of educators, reading specialists, and content developers around five essential components—phonemic awareness, phonics, vocabulary, text comprehension, and fluency—to assist young readers as they develop reading skills and strategies and increase their general knowledge. All books are written, reviewed, and leveled for guided reading, early reading intervention, and Accelerated Reader® programs for use in shared, guided, and independent reading and writing activities to support a balanced approach to literacy instruction. The SandCastle™ series has four levels that correspond to early literacy development. The levels help teachers and parents select appropriate books for young readers.

Emerging Readers
(no flags)

Beginning Readers
(1 flag)

Transitional Readers
(2 flags)

Fluent Readers
(3 flags)

These levels are meant only as a guide. All levels are subject to change.

Data is factual information about something. Data comes from observing or measuring something. Data is collected during an investigation.

Words used to talk about data:

chart	information
graph	number
how many	pattern
how much	

I collect data when

I count the number

of in a tree.

Measuring how much 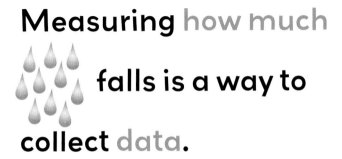 falls is a way to collect data.

Writing down how many hours I is a way to collect data .

I can record information

in a [notebook].

I can make a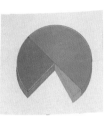

to show data.

I can draw a to show data.

I'll Use Information for My Explanation!

Birds I Saw at the Park

Robins

Cardinals

Bluejays

There is a girl named Gretchen who gathers data and information. It's the foundation for her explanation.

I will start by making a chart!

Birds I Saw at the Park

 Robins

‖‖‖ |

 Cardinals

|||

 Bluejays

||

Gretchen is pleased
by the number
of birds she sees.
She isn't bored
by what she can record.

I use numbers
to learn
if there's a pattern!

Birds I Saw at the Park

Robins

||||| ||| ⑧

Cardinals

||||| ④

Bluejays

||||| ⑤

Gretchen has collected and inspected the information for her explanation.

I proved what I heard. The robin is the most common bird!

15

We Use Data Every Day!

Caleb's team has six wins and three losses.

The record of how many wins and losses a sports team has is one kind of data.

4' 8"

4' 3"

18

Becky has grown four inches since her birthday last year.

Keeping track of how much something changes is another way to collect data.

Gina and Ella count how many parrots live at the zoo.

Writing down how many there are of something is collecting data.

Nick keeps a journal to record information about the fruits and vegetables that he eats during the day.

What other kinds of data can you think of?

Glossary

foundation – the basis for something.

inspect – to look at closely.

investigation – a careful search or study done to learn facts about something.

journal – a record of your thoughts and observations.

observe – to watch carefully.

pattern – a combination of characteristics that repeat in a recognizable way.

record – to write down.